The Wreck

of the

Santa Maria

Bill Haynie

What I discovered beneath the Caribbean sands could rewrite history and reveal what really happened to Columbus's flagship.

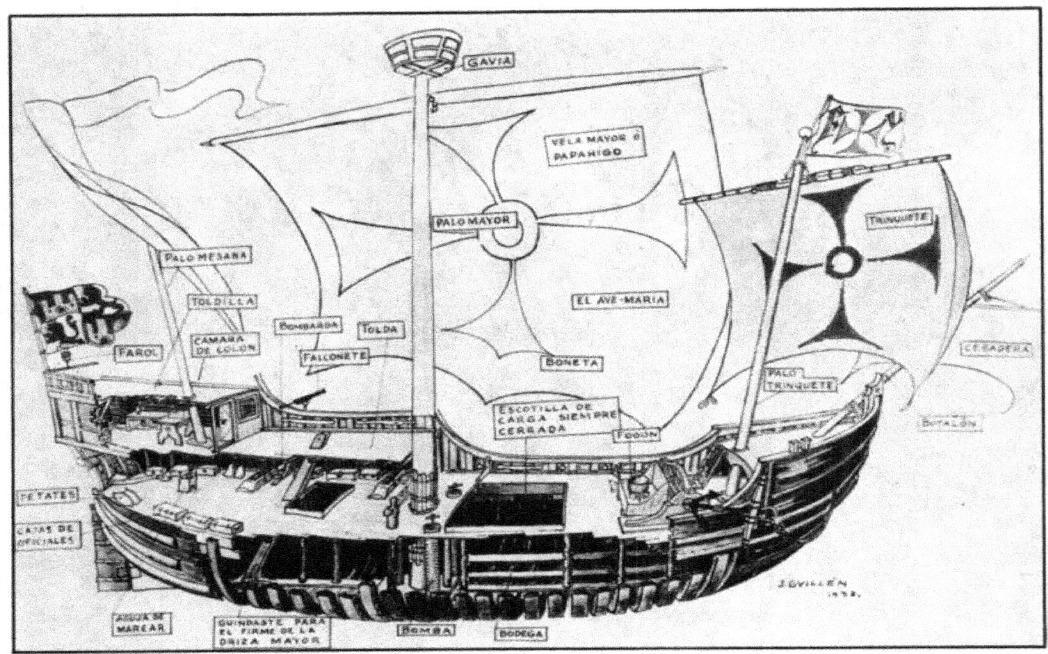

Santa Maria

Table of Contents

Chapter One

The year was 1492, and the open sea stretched endlessly before Christopher Columbus and his fleet—three ships riding the restless Atlantic like specks on a boundless canvas. The Santa María, the largest of the trio, creaked under the strain of saltwater winds and the weight of European ambition. Her sails snapped taut as the trade winds nudged the expedition westward, toward what Columbus believed would be the spice-laden shores of Asia.

After weeks of monotony and fear among the crew, a cry finally pierced the salty air: "Tierra! Land!" Spirits soared as the coast of what we now know as the Bahamas shimmered on the horizon. Columbus, triumphant, stepped ashore, planting the Spanish flag into the soft sand. But destiny, as unpredictable as the sea itself, was not finished with the Santa María.

On the night of December 5, 1492, the *Santa María* rode the land breeze along Hispaniola's northern coast. By dawn, Columbus had taken his bearings with uncanny precision—so precise that modern charts confirm his notes placed the flagship twelve miles north by east of Cape St. Nicholas Mole. For a man squinting across a crude compass card, it was an astonishing feat of seamanship.

From that position, he sighted Tortuga, the buccaneers' island, and to the east a towering slope he named Cabo de la Lefante.

By December 6, the *Santa María* entered a harbor Columbus christened Puerto de San Nicolás. He declared it the finest port he had yet seen—deep, sheltered, with a clean bottom and firm holding ground. He envisioned it as a future stronghold of the empire. Days later, on December 12, he raised a great cross on the western cape of what we now call Moustique Bay, formally claiming Hispaniola for Ferdinand and Isabella.

The encounter with the islanders soon followed. An old man spoke of distant islands filled with gold—so much that it was gathered like sand, smelted into bars, hammered into ornaments. Columbus, already obsessed, was inflamed. Whether the man had described real smelting in Costa Rica or whether Columbus had misread gestures made little difference. To the Admiral, the promise of gold lay east, and he set sail that very night.

At sunrise on December 20, he discovered a bay of such beauty that words failed him. Even Bartolomé de las Casas, recounting Columbus's awestruck journal, admitted the Admiral seemed embarrassed by his own excess of praise. Columbus named it the Bay of St. Thomas; today, I call it Acul Bay. Protected by high headlands and calm in all weathers, it remains one of the loveliest harbors in the world. I myself would come to know it well, a place of deep calm amid Haiti's rugged coast.

But the entrance was treacherous, barred by reefs. Columbus had to feel his way in by lead line, leaving directions that sailors can still follow: align with a wooded island at the head of the harbor, steer straight, favor the eastern channel, and pass within a Lombard shot of the shore. A Lombard—an early cannon—was the very signal gun that had once cried "Land!" in the Bahamas.

By sunset, only the *Santa María* and the *Niña* lay at anchor. The *Pinta* had deserted weeks before, lured eastward by rumors of gold.

The next day, December 21, Columbus sent men inland. They returned with news of a nearby village. Soon, the shore swarmed with islanders offering cassava bread, calabashes, water, and earthen vessels. They traded gold pieces as casually as food. In return, Columbus's men gave trinkets—beads, cloth, hawks' bells—and took as much gold as their hands could hold. The Admiral, convinced that greater riches lay farther east, ordered sail at dawn.

But strong winds forced him back, anchoring again near the mouth of Acul Bay. There, a messenger arrived from Guacanagarí, chief of the region. He bore a gift unlike anything Columbus had ever seen: a cotton girdle embroidered with red and white fishbones, four fingers wide, so stiff and strong it could turn a musket shot. At its center, a mask gleamed—nose, ears, and tongue beaten in hammered gold.

The Admiral's obsession was now unstoppable. The currents of greed, myth, and destiny were sweeping him—and his flagship—toward their fateful end.

As Christmas Eve of that same year approached, the Santa María sailed near the northern coast of present-day Haiti. The night was serene, the ocean deceptively calm. Exhausted from months at sea, the crew's vigilance waned. Columbus, too, had retired to his cabin, trusting the ship to a young cabin boy.

Then came the shuddering lurch—a sudden, grinding scrape as the keel struck a hidden reef. Sailors scrambled to their posts, hearts pounding. The Santa María was stuck fast, her timbers groaning as waves pummeled her hull. Panic gripped the crew as they fought to salvage supplies and navigate the perilous waters.

Despite their efforts, the mighty ship could not be saved. By dawn, the realization settled over them like a heavy fog: the Santa María was lost. Columbus, ever the pragmatist, ordered her remains stripped. Timber was used to build a small settlement named La Navidad—the first European foothold in the New World.

The wreck of the Santa María marked a turning point. Though the ship met a watery grave, Columbus's voyage had forever changed the course of history. Europe's eyes were now fixed on these "new" lands, and the age of exploration had truly begun.

If the Santa Maria had not grounded on that Christmas day, we Americans probably would not be here as we are today.

Chapter Two

I was an internationally known professional treasure hunter, rather a treasure finder. I was known from Mexico to the Antilles. Having lived in the Bahamas islands, Haiti, the British Virgin Islands, and the Cayman Islands, I have dived on the reefs and wrecks throughout the Caribbean. I spent most of my life in the Florida Keys, where my early years were spent learning about sunken and buried treasures. I worked with Mel Fisher of Atocha fame, tested treasure hunting equipment with Burt Webber of Conception fame, and explored jungles in the Cayman Islands with Winston McDermot, a charter diving entrepreneur. AII of his close friends are prospectors or treasure finders as well. I searched for and found Spanish mines in Utah and Mexico. Walked and explored the Nevada, Arizona, Utah, and California deserts with Cal Johnson, a mining man from South America.

Built gold recovery equipment with Jim King, a recovery systems genius from Arizona. I have been hunting and finding treasure for over 60 years. I have secrets, many, many secrets. The best secret I have kept for 55 years will be revealed in the pages of this book. Secrets for treasure hunters usually are not long in duration, due to the nature of the breed. Professional treasure finders are secretive for many reasons, but long, I and bound seasons loosen tongues. And bragging is a form of therapy for hot, windy days in the deserts of the American Southwest. The secret of the Santa Maria is truly a great piece of archeological detective work that all should thoroughly enjoy.

Chapter Three

I was born in Birmingham, Alabama to a policeman father and a registered nurse mother, and was groomed by grandparents and many aunts and uncles. I served my country in the U S Coast Guard and was a cadet in the Civil Air Patrol where I earned many honors. One being nominated to the very first class of the U.S. Air Force Academy. An ear problem kept me out of consideration for the Academy. I also learned to identify aircraft in the air and on the ground.

Married in 1961, I was the father of a daughter and son, and living in Miami, Florida, in 1963. My early professional background was rooted in engineering and steel fabrication. I worked on the ground support equipment for the Jupiter C missile, the rocket that launched America's first satellite. I got my first taste of mining equipment while working in the engineering department of a foundry that built rock crushing equipment and dredge pumps. My technical background led to a production planning job at Bertram Yacht Co. in Miami.

Chapter Four

After moving to Miami, I later opened a dive shop. I was close to the Florida Keys, so I would dive in the upper Keys region. I found or was shown many wrecks in the area. Some of these wrecks were Spanish, and some were British.

The Spanish shipwrecks were mostly from the hurricane of 1733. There were about twenty of them in shallow water. I spent a lot of time on several of these wrecks.

Now, one thing is important for everyone to understand about wooden hull ships. After about 50 years, most of the wood above the ballast was eaten by worms. So only metal and ballast would be left to show that a wreck was present. The ballast was mostly round river rocks from some rivers in Spain. The metals would be cannons, anchors, and some rigging (on the masts).

Some of the wrecks were completely covered with sand in places, while others were exposed on the bottom. There was not much coral growth on these shipwrecks, as they had mostly passed over the reef areas.

My experiences diving on these wrecks brought me into contact with a lot of salvage divers. One of these was a group from Freeport Grand

Bahamas who had found what they thought was a Spanish shipwreck just a few hundred yards off the coast near Freeport. The person who had found this wreck came to Miami to talk with me about coming to the Bahamas to help their salvage team. While he was in Miami, I thought it would be worthwhile to take him to one of my sites to see what he knew about salvage work. He was not that experienced in salvage work.

I then decided to take him up on his offer. I left my dive shop in the care of my wife. I then went to Freeport to meet the team. There were five people who had been hired by the company that had been formed after the wreck was found. Four of them were divers, and one was a cook.

We were staying on a large private yacht that belonged to a very wealthy person who had left Miami to avoid large taxes on his business. This vessel was well equipped with large staterooms, and a large dining area.

We worked two shifts per day, about two hours per shift. Sometimes we worked seven days in a row. The salvage work was quite easy. On breaks we would spear fish for food.

Chapter Five

That's where I met Fred Dixon, a member of the Explorers Club. He would become a major actor in this story.

Fred belonged to the prestigious Explorers Club out of New York. He had credentials in adventure, but when it came to shipwreck salvage, especially on old wooden-hull vessels, he was still green. He and I shared a cabin aboard the yacht, and over time, we became good friends. Fred was eager to learn, and I was more than willing to show him the ropes.

While we worked the wreck site, I introduced Fred to proper salvage techniques using the equipment we had at the time. Back then, we used long metal tubes—sort of homemade dredges—connected to surface air pumps. These tubes had air hoses running inside them, creating a high-pressure stream at the bottom. That blast of air created suction, like a giant underwater vacuum.

We'd aim the bottom of the tube at the sand, and the high-velocity bubbles would lift sediment, exposing anything buried beneath. It wasn't fancy, but it worked. And when you're uncovering hundreds of years of history, every inch of cleared bottom counts.

Fred caught on quickly. He was smart and observant, and while he might not have had a background in shipwreck salvage, he understood the gravity of what we were doing.

The wreck we'd found wasn't Spanish. It was a pirate ship. One of Piet Hein's vessels—a Dutch privateer who captured the Spanish fleet off Cuba in 1628. Thousands of silver coins were stolen. One of his ships wrecked in the Bahamas that same year.

We believed we'd found it.

We recovered over 20,000 silver coins, two cannons, and one anchor. Coins were fused to the cannons—likely stowed together. The ship had clearly broken up after striking the reef. We were picking up so many coins daylily, and we all kept some personally. There was a bar in Freeport that we frequently went to. Now, back then, those coins would be worth about $150 each. We would tip the barmaids and cocktail waitresses with coins. I noticed that the wreck was not intact. My knowledge of very old wrecks led me to believe this was only a small part of the ship. I also learned from a local that there have been coins of the same year found north of where we were working.. After a few more weeks, I returned to Florida.

Chapter Six

A hurricane had just passed through Florida, and dozens of boats were sunk. I started salvaging vessels for the owners. I checked on some of the old wrecks I knew in the Keys. One was the San Pedro, from the 1733 fleet. I'd been there many times. The wreck was not disturbed by the hurricane. I found some artifacts right on the surface of the ship.

Then, one day, I opened the Miami Herald.

There it was. An article by Fred Dixon.

He claimed to have found the remains of the Santa María off the north coast of Haiti. He said someone had shown him a site—claimed it was the legendary shipwreck.

I froze. Because I knew Fred. And I knew shipwrecks.

And I knew something wasn't right.

I read the article twice. The location mentioned was off the northern coast of Haiti—exactly where Columbus's logs claimed the Santa María had run aground. Fred said a local had shown him the wreck. He described old timber, iron fittings, and some ballast stones. No cannons, no cargo, no identifying features.

I knew what a centuries-old wooden wreck looked like. I also knew how unreliable some locals could be when a dollar or two dangled in front of them. And Fred—well, he meant well, but he wasn't an expert in identifying 15th-century wreckage.

Fred told of artifacts that he had found on the shipwreck, and I knew that it could not be the Santa Maria.

I had read a lot about that fateful day when the Santa Maria was lost on the north coast of Haiti. Columbus had his men completely dismantle the flagship to build a small fort on land. There would not be too much left of that vessel that would provide artifacts that Fred had said that he had found.

I told Fred this, and he said that he had to prove this because he had founded the Santa Maria Foundation. I told him to go for it. That was the proper thing to do.

A short time later, a friend that I had known when I worked as an activities director in the Virgin Islands came to me in Miami about a boat that he had for sale. The vessel was a 200-foot passenger ship without an engine. It was steel with everything working inside. The selling price was very low, so my uncle and I bought it.

Our thinking was to tow the vessel to La. And break it up for salvage. There was a lot of copper and steel in and on her, so we could make a nice profit. It had many objects that could be salvaged, such as beds, tables, and chairs in very good condition.

I moved out of my apartment and onto the ship. Everything I needed was available on board: a Full kitchen, a nice bathroom, good bedroom layout.

I was salvaging some of the copper to pay for my time on board. There was good money there.

One day, a gentleman came to the ship and wanted to talk with me about an idea that he had. He said that his family had exclusive rights to all casino operations in Haiti. His idea was for us to tow the ship to Haiti and turn it into a floating casino. We jumped all over that.

I brought two young men on board to help with the set-up for the tow, and they both stated that they would like to stay on board for the tow.

I found a boat in the Miami River that the crew said they would gladly tow the ship to Haiti.

Chapter Seven

The tow boat was not strong enough to tow a 200 ft. ship thru the Straits between Cuba and the lower Bahama islands. I suggested that we go up and around the northern part of the Bahamas and come down the east side. That worked well.

This was not a fast tow; in fact, we were going quite slow. However, the water was smooth and no wind hampered us. It was just long days and nights.

I remember reading in Columbus' journal that on the night before they made landfall in the Bahamas, he and two of his men were standing on the deck of the Santa Maria. They all noticed two lights come up out of the water and go back down. Eventually, we were towed into that area.

The three of us were standing on the fantail (rear of ship) at night, with clear skies and calm waters. I looked down into the depts and saw a small bright light begin to rise. As it got closer to the surface, it expanded in size that completely covered the width of ship. I had spent a lot of time in, on, and under the oceans of the Caribbean. There was nothing that I knew about that would do that. It continued to rise, expand and descend again and again. Now we were being towed at a pace of around six knots. That light stayed exactly on the back of the ship where we were standing.

The boys became frightened and went below to their cabins, and I stayed to watch for quite a while, eventually going back to my stateroom. I had several marine scientists in Miami that I had provided with tropical fish for study. I later contacted them about the lights and was told that there was nothing known to them that would do what we had seen. Another incident occurred that almost blew me away.

The tow boat was running low on fuel, so the captain decided to head for the nearest island to top off. He took us around one of the larger islands to the south and anchored our vessel, the *Holliday*, in what looked like shallow water on the island's west side. Then the tow boat headed in for fuel. I went along so I could call my family, and one of the boys came with us.

It took longer than expected to get the fuel, so we decided to spend the night on the island. The next morning, we returned to pick up the *Holliday*. As we turned into the back side of the island where she'd been anchored, I froze in disbelief—she was gone! Vanished. Not a trace of her anywhere.

I couldn't believe it. How could a 200-foot ship just disappear overnight? The tow line was several hundred feet long, enough for the anchor to catch in shallow water. But just beyond that, the bottom dropped off into deep water. My stomach sank as I thought, *How in hell am I going to tell my uncle I lost the ship?*

We continued north along the coast, stopping at villages to ask if anyone had seen her. Finally, someone said they'd seen a large vessel drifting north over deep water. I called the Coast Guard in Miami and asked for help. They sent a plane, and before long they radioed back—our ship had been spotted farther up the coast, riding at anchor.

When we reached her, the *Holliday* was resting stern-first in shallow water on a reef—but miraculously, she wasn't wrecked. The tow boat simply hadn't anchored her properly. After that scare, the rest of the tow went smoothly. We had no more incidents that could compare with *the lights*, and at last we reached Cap-Haïtien, Haiti.

Chapter Eight

The ship was tied up at the dock in Cap-Haïtien, and I wasted no time hiring workers to restore her. Some spoke English, some did not, but it didn't matter—they worked together like a seasoned crew. I grew close to many of them. Back then, the people of Haiti were kind, welcoming, and full of life.

The family I was involved with had an unusual history. They had once owned casinos in Cuba, later in the Bahamas, and now they had established themselves in Haiti. Through them, I was introduced to many people, one of whom would become very important in my time there.

He was a pilot who flew important people across the country in two small twin-engine planes. Whenever I needed to travel to the capital, he would offer me a seat. In return, I helped him keep the planes flying—lining up mechanics and parts so he didn't have to ferry the aircraft back to the States every time something broke. We often flew to Florida as well: he on personal business, me to gather supplies for my ship.

One trip still stands out. We were flying back from Port-au-Prince to Cap-Haitien, skimming over the mountains as a thick blanket of cloud built up ahead. Soon we were inside it—white everywhere, no ground, no horizon. I was navigating for my friend, head down in the charts, when suddenly he said, "Bill, I've got vertigo—I can't see clearly!"

I sat up fast and grabbed the wheel, but like a fool I glanced outside. The world spun and vertigo hit me too. For a moment, both of us were lost in that endless white, and I'll never forget the sickening weight of it. Then, mercifully, his vision cleared. He took back the controls, leveled us out, and moments later we broke free of the cloud into sunlight and sea. The coast stretched below us like salvation, and soon we were down safe in Cap-Haitien.

My pilot friend and I decided to fly back to Miami one night to get supplies and visit family. Again, I was navigating for the trip. We had flown this several times together, and we were familiar with our surroundings.

Flying was second nature to me. My mother had been a pilot, and I'd been at the controls of airplanes since I was young. I knew the sky, I knew its rules — and I knew when something wasn't right.

One night, we left Haiti in the dark, headed for Miami. We'd traveled a long way and were nearing Florida, but still in the vast reach of the Bermuda Triangle, when the first sign of trouble appeared. The cockpit instruments began to spin wildly, needles twitching, readings rolling over as if the gauges had lost their minds.

My friend, at the controls, told me to call Miami tower and see if they had us on radar. I picked up the mic and transmitted, "Miami, do you have Seven-Zero-Zero Romeo in sight?"

The tower came back: "Sorry Seven-Zero-Zero Romeo, we don't see you. Make a ninety-degree right turn and hit your IFF."

I reached over and pressed the IFF button — the transponder signal pilots send to identify their aircraft. Moments later, the tower's voice returned: "We have you now, Seven-Zero-Zero Romeo. Turn back to the airport. We'll set you up for landing."

I had barely released the mic when the voice came back, this time urgent, almost shouting: "Seven-Zero-Zero Romeo, dive, dive NOW!"

We pushed the yoke forward just as a massive, silent triangle-shaped craft passed directly over us. It blotted out the stars for a heartbeat, a shadow bigger than anything I'd ever seen in the air, sliding past without a sound. Then it was gone, leaving only the hiss of the radio and our own breathing. The craft flew down into the ocean in the area where I had encountered the lights underwater..

Several months later, we were talking about the incident when we decided to go to the Miami airport tower to see if we could get a copy of the audio of the event. We took my friends log book with all of the information about that incident with us. We gave one of the operators the info, and he said I will be right back with that for you. He did not come right back, in fact it was quite a while before he came back, When the operator returned, he did not look at us bur said bluntly, "We don't have that tape".

When I was a boy, my father told me stories most people would never dare speak aloud. He had known about UFO crashes as far back as 1947, and he shared that knowledge with me quietly, almost as if he were preparing me for a world the rest of society would never accept. Long before I ever sailed or flew over the Bermuda Triangle, I carried his words with me—a private certainty that there was far more to our skies and seas than anyone admitted publicly.

Years later, I heard a story that echoed everything he had warned me about. A lady friend of mine made her living moving boats for owners, delivering them from one port to another. One evening, she and her boyfriend were tasked with sailing a small boat from the Bahamas back to Miami. She told me the story herself.

They left Bimini after dark, expecting the trip to take six hours in good weather. Not long offshore, a strange cloud rose from the sea, thick and glowing in the night. With no way around it, they pressed forward.

Inside, everything changed. The sails, the rigging—even their own skin—lit up with an unearthly glow. She said it felt like the boat itself was alive. They were stunned, but they kept sailing, and within minutes the cloud lifted.

When the haze cleared, they were no longer off Bimini. They were in Miami waters. A voyage of six hours had vanished into ten minutes.

Her story stayed with me because by then I had already seen strange things myself in the Triangle. One night, while being towed, a brilliant light moved silently beneath the water's surface, keeping pace with us as if we were being observed. No one aboard could explain it.

Chapter Nine

Fred Dixon arrived in Cap-Haïtien while I was working on the ship. We met and talked often about the location where he believed the wreck lay. He had rented a house from a friend of mine whose family owned a beautiful resort in the hills above town. A local man was keeping a salvage boat for Fred in the harbor, but before his return, a storm had swept through and destroyed it.

I helped him find another vessel—this one a houseboat owned by a tourist who wanted to join in Fred's search. It was far from a proper salvage boat, but it gave him a way to stay on the water.

While I traveled to the capital to meet with the family who had brought me to Haiti, Fred pressed on with his diving. He had one great fear: jellyfish. One day, at his site, he climbed to the top deck of the houseboat and peered over the side to check for them before diving in.

When he leapt, his mask hit the water head-on. The force drove the frame into his skull, breaking a plate of bone just above his nose. He came up bleeding heavily and was rushed back to his house.

I returned from the capital soon after and went straight to him. He lay in bed, a wastebasket beside him filled with dark clotted blood. He told me a doctor had seen him but could do nothing. A transfusion was scheduled for the following morning.

A cruise ship was due to dock the next day, and I told Fred I would see him safely aboard in Miami. But I insisted he get that transfusion first.

At dawn, someone knocked at my door. A friend staying at a nearby hotel stood there with grim news: Fred had died in the night.

I was devastated.

I made arrangements for his body to be taken to a funeral home owned by another friend. There I saw him one last time—his skin pale yellow in death. That evening, we carried his body to the cruise ship and loaded him into the cargo hold. Before we left, I tossed silver coins into the dark harbor waters—a tribute to a diver lost too soon.

The grief weighed on me heavily. It was hard to adjust to the sudden emptiness of his absence.

Chapter Ten

There is a hotel high above the city of Cap-Haïtien, owned by my friend Walter. His family had held it for generations. From its patio, you could see the harbor spread out below—cruise ships, fishing boats, and the constant bustle of the Caribbean trade. Sitting there, watching the harbor's movement, was always an experience.

One afternoon, Walter joined me on the patio. He pointed toward a shallow reef that jutted out from the mainland into the harbor.

"When I was a boy," he said, "mangroves grew out there. Since then, people have cut them down for charcoal."

His words struck me. Why did that reef extend so far out now? If mangroves had once grown thick atop land jutting into the harbor, then the harbor must have been almost closed at one time. I pressed him for more, but he only smiled and said, "My mother has a book that may interest you."

The book was an old French volume, *Travels of a Frenchman*, written by Moreau de Saint-Méry. Walter loaned it to me, and in its pages I found a fascinating account of Cap-Haïtien's harbor in the 1730s. Saint-Méry described how ships had to sail past the harbor before turning back to make their entrance. That was not the harbor I knew. Today the entrance is wide, visible from thirty miles away. But on Saint-Méry's day, the mangroves had grown thick, nearly concealing the opening.

The changes in the land intrigued me. What had caused them?

I took my questions to Father Roland Lamy, a Catholic priest I knew in Cap-Haïtien. He suggested we seek out Dr. Hodges, a medical missionary with a clinic at Bord de Mer de Limonade, near the very place Columbus had established *La Navidad* after the wreck of the Santa María in 1492.

Dr. Hodges greeted us warmly. To my surprise, he was not only a doctor but also an amateur archaeologist who had studied Columbus for years. Locals often brought him artifacts, which he traced back to their find spots. Piece by piece, he had reconstructed a picture of where *La Navidad* might have stood.

He had even erected a stone monument at the site—commemorating Columbus's landfall on Christmas Day, 1492.

When he led us there, something immediately caught my eye. The monument was half-buried in level sand, as if the ground itself had been rising around it for years. To me, that spoke volumes about the shifting coastline, erosion, and sediment buildup. At first, Father Lamy did not grasp the weight of what I pointed out. But when we returned to Cap-Haïtien, he began searching Vatican sources for maps and records, while I turned to modern charts and surveys.

Two paths of research—both aimed at unraveling the secret of the land, the sea, and the hidden wreck of the Santa María.

Please understand that Haiti is a very poor country—probably the poorest in the Western Hemisphere. The needs are great, and the people lack many of the essentials we take for granted. One of the things they don't have is fuel for cooking or heating their homes—or huts, as many of them live in. For that, they rely heavily on charcoal fires.

Most of their meats are braised, so charcoal is necessary for preparing food. Unfortunately, the source of that charcoal is the country's once-abundant hardwood trees. In the past, the forests were thick and healthy, but over time, they've been cut down to feed the charcoal industry. As the hardwoods high in the mountains are harvested, the forests are stripped bare. And in a land like Haiti—where mountains are steep and rainfall is heavy—that deforestation comes with devastating consequences.

Without the trees to anchor the soil, the fertile top layer is washed away into the rivers, carried downstream to the deltas, and finally dumped into the sea. Once the topsoil is gone, there's nothing left to hold vegetation, which means no plants to retain moisture, no clouds to form, and no rain to fall. With little rainfall, the smaller rivers run dry, leaving behind empty beds where water once flowed. Only the major rivers remain, and even they struggle under the strain.

Along the Haitian-Dominican border, rivers like the Massacre and the Grand Rivière du Nord continue to carry what soil is left, often in sudden floods that threaten what little crops the farmers have managed to grow. The cycle is cruel and unrelenting.

To survive, Haitian farmers resort to slash-and-burn agriculture. They cut and burn whatever land they can, planting quickly before the rains strip it bare again. Each storm takes more of the soil away, leaving less behind for the next crop. Year after year, the cycle repeats—until the land is barren, the rivers choked with silt, and the ocean itself claiming the earth that once sustained life.

Chapter Eleven

While diving off Tortuga Island, just north of Haiti, I came across something that stopped me cold—an anchor so massive I could have driven a Volkswagen clean through the shackle hole. The sheer size of it spoke of an era long gone, a relic from a ship of incredible weight and purpose. I hovered there in the dim green light, running my hand along the coral-encrusted iron, wondering what stories it could tell if it could speak. Tortuga had seen its share of pirates and explorers, but this anchor seemed older, heavier—as if it belonged to another age entirely.

On the north side of the island, I later found the scattered remains of a shipwreck lying just outside a small bay called Treasure Harbor. The name itself felt like something out of a legend, and in a way, it was. Years earlier, I had come across an old account describing how pirates had attacked a Spanish ship laden with silver in that very area. Standing on the deck of my dive boat, looking toward the jungle-covered shoreline, I couldn't help but feel that I was staring straight into the pages of history— right where it had actually happened.

I actually found shipwrecks all along the north coast of Haiti. The local fishermen—many of them free divers who hunted lobster and fish— told me stories of wrecks scattered beneath those waters. They'd seen timbers, cannons, and anchors resting in the sand where history itself had gone to sleep. I lived aboard my ship in Cap-Haïtien, diving for fish and lobster whenever I wasn't hunting wrecks. One morning, in the crystal-clear water of the harbor, I found it—a massive, long-forgotten hulk resting on the bottom. Over ninety iron cannons lay across its deck, blackened with age, still aimed toward the mountains. They weren't meant to attack passing ships—they had been forged for Henri Christophe's fort, perched high above the coast, to rain fire on any enemy daring to approach. Hovering above that silent arsenal, I felt the weight of centuries pressing down, a reminder that the past never truly sinks.

And yet, as compelling as this harbor wreck was, it was only a prelude. My true obsession lay elsewhere—deep beneath the waves where the Santa María had finally slipped into history. Every dive, every discovery, every echo of iron and wood, led me closer to the wreck that had haunted maps and legends for centuries. The cannons in the harbor were a warning from the past; the Santa María was a challenge, calling me to uncover what time had buried.

Chapter Twelve

The Legend of El Dorado

There's a stretch of sea between Hispaniola and Puerto Rico called the Mona Passage — deep, blue, and treacherous. Sailors say it's haunted, and maybe they're right. I've always believed the ocean remembers what man forgets.

It was July 4th, 1502, when fate decided to even the score. A fleet of thirty-two caravels lay at anchor in Santo Domingo, ready to sail for Spain. Among the passengers on Antonio de Torres's flagship, *El Dorado*, was none other than Francisco de Bobadilla — the same man who had thrown Christopher Columbus in chains just two years before.

By a strange twist, Columbus himself happened to be in port that day. He studied the sky, felt the heavy stillness in the air — the kind of quiet only an old sailor understands. He warned Bobadilla that a hurricane was coming. But Bobadilla, swollen with pride and gold, laughed it off.

Four days later, nature answered.

The hurricane struck with a fury no one had ever seen. For twelve endless hours, it ripped across the Caribbean — winds screaming like demons, waves rising as high as towers. The fleet was torn apart. Some ships vanished into the depths; others were shattered on reefs and beaches from Santo Domingo to Puerto Rico.

When the sea finally fell silent, only five ships remained. Twenty-seven were gone — among them *El Dorado*, swallowed whole by the Mona Passage with more than five hundred souls.

And she didn't go down empty. The fleet had been heavy with treasure — gold dust, pearls, and the spoils of a New World. Half of it, they say, was aboard *El Dorado*. The prize of them all was a solid gold table — one and a half tons of it — that Bobadilla planned to gift to the Catholic Monarchs in thanks for his power.

Instead, it became his coffin lid.

No diver, no salvager, no dreamer has ever brought back so much as a splinter of *El Dorado*. The Mona Passage drops a thousand feet there — dark water, cold and unforgiving. After the storm, salvors found gold scattered on the beaches, but millions in treasure simply vanished.

Somewhere down there, beneath centuries of shifting sand and coral, lies Bobadilla's golden table — the symbol of a man's arrogance and the ocean's justice.

I've often thought of that wreck when I've been over deep water, feeling the currents whisper against my mask. *El Dorado* was more than a ship — she was a warning. The sea gives nothing freely, and when it takes, it keeps. I know people who have found that wreck.

But now, back to my real search.

Father Lamy had obtained ancient maps from the Vatican—documents few people even knew existed. I had my own topographical charts of the region, and together we began comparing them. That's when we noticed something extraordinary.

On one of Father Lamy's old maps, there appeared a small reef close to shore—right in the area where the *Santa María* had reportedly gone aground. But when I looked at my modern topo map, that reef was gone.

I overlaid both maps and marked the modern landmarks. The truth hit us at once: the wreck site would have been on that reef.

And that reef—according to today's geography—was now buried *miles inland*.

That was the proof. The *Santa María* wasn't lost at sea—she was entombed beneath the very earth of northern Haiti.

I'd been around countless wreck sites in my life, but never had I seen anything like this. A shipwreck buried under land! Father Lamy and I just looked at each other and smiled. We finally knew why the *Santa María* had never been found.

I kept that revelation to myself for many years. Others came after, claiming they'd found her—but sorry, gentlemen, not even close.

Epilogue

Several years after I had returned to Florida from Haiti, life took me south again. I moved to the Florida Keys to care for my mother, trading one shoreline for another. During that time, a well-known treasure-hunting magazine featured a story about my adventures. Not long after, a man from the Cayman Islands reached out. He had read about me and wanted me to join a search based on information he claimed to have. His name was Winston McDermot.

Winston was no stranger to the Caribbean. He had spent years moving between the islands before settling on Cayman Brac, where he was raising a family. He owned a magnificent boat—purpose-built for serious diving expeditions. When I arrived on the Brac, he welcomed me aboard and immediately put the vessel through its paces. We sailed to Little Cayman and anchored off the north shore.

Little Cayman had always been steeped in legend. For generations it had been whispered about as a pirate stronghold. Raiders had terrorized shipping lanes from there, and eventually the Jamaican government had enough. They dispatched several warships to eradicate the problem. Two ships stormed the southern shore at South Hole Sound, where the main pirate camp lay, while another cut off escape from the north. Only one pirate slipped away. He fled to Central America, built a life there, and passed down stories of what had been hidden on Little Cayman.

Centuries later, one of his descendants reached out to an American with tales of buried treasure. Together they came to the island, guided by a local man who warned them: "The island will not let you take anything." They left empty-handed.

When Winston and I prepared to go ashore, he told me something curious. He claimed a psychic had warned him never to hunt treasure on Little Cayman because of the deaths that had occurred there. I brushed it off. "There's no danger," I said.

I was wrong.

The island was like nothing I had ever seen—dense jungle, swampy ground, the kind of place that swallows you whole. It was the middle of summer and brutally hot. We carried as much water as we could and left it in one central location for everyone to access.

I pushed into the jungle alone, cutting a path through vines and low branches. After a while, parched from the heat, I turned back to get water. I knew I was only a few yards away. Passing a gumbo limbo tree, I walked on—only to circle back to that same tree minutes later. Confused, I tried again. Once more, I ended up at the same tree.

Finally, I climbed it to get my bearings. That's when it happened.

A voice—clear, deep, and male—spoke from nowhere: "I told you not to come down here."

I nearly lost my grip. Heart pounding, I scanned the jungle. In the distance, I could see the others at the water site. None of them had spoken.

When I told them what I'd heard, the color drained from their faces. Without another word, they insisted we leave. We packed up and got off that island fast. But I went back. Many times. And that is another story.

Wreck of The Santa Maria

Ballast

EL POPULO BALLAST

The last two pics are what a shipwreck looks like after about 50 years.

What I discovered beneath the Caribbean sands could rewrite history and reveal what really happened to Columbus's flagship.